The Case of the Adder that Didn't Add Up

T0318113

Written by Chris Bradford

Illustrated by Sarah Horne

Collins

1 The Body

Detective Snooper sniffed at the mouse's body lying in the middle of the burrow, then prodded it with his snout. His eyesight poor, the hedgehog began to examine the lifeless mouse with a large magnifying glass.

A red squirrel burst into the burrow. Her bushy tail swept the ceiling, knocked a picture from the wall, then a vase off the sideboard. Spinning round, she caught the vase ... but her tail snagged on the tablecloth and sent plates and cutlery smashing to the floor.

"Sorry I'm late, Detective Snooper," panted the squirrel. She put the vase back and sheepishly dusted the sideboard.

"Who are you?" the hedgehog demanded.

The squirrel stuck out a paw and beamed. "Sly, your new partner!"

Detective Snooper narrowed his beady eyes. "I work alone."

"Not anymore," Sly replied, her grin widening.

Snooper ignored Sly's outstretched paw and turned back to the body.

Sly's smile dropped. Then she noticed the cobweb stuck to her paw and wiped it away. "Oh dear ... mustn't contaminate the crime scene."

"Too late," Snooper grunted. With a sigh, he continued his inspection. "No footprints ... No blood ... No obvious weapon ..." He glanced at Sly. "Why aren't you taking notes?"

"Sorry, Detective!" Sly grabbed her notepad.

Snooper rolled the mouse over and peered closely with the magnifying glass. "Two small wounds to the neck … five millimetres apart … very interesting …" He picked up what looked to Sly like a brown sliver of broken plate. "The criminal was clearly disturbed in the middle of the attack—"

"How do you know?" asked Sly.

"Well, the victim *hasn't* been eaten!" Snooper squinted at the squirrel. "Are you *sure* you're a detective?"

Sly nodded. "I just qualified! So, what shall I put down as time of death?"

Snooper frowned. "Death?"

"Yes, as in ... *urghh*—" Sly made a face and stuck out a lolling tongue.

"The victim *isn't* dead," Snooper said. "Poisoned and paralysed, maybe, but not dead ... not yet anyway." He felt the mouse's pulse. "I need to figure out which animal poisoned her, otherwise Molly has perhaps 24 hours left to live. After that, this *will* be a murder case."

Sly's eyes widened. "Then we must work fast – a mouse's life is at stake!"

2 The Legend

As Snooper and Sly emerged from the burrow, Officer Beck was questioning a vole next door.

"You heard an argument, then someone leave by the back door?" asked the otter.

"Yes," sobbed the tiny vole, dabbing her eyes with a hanky.

Snooper stared hard at the mouse's neighbour. "*Who* left?"

"I-I-I don't know," replied the vole. "I couldn't see them over the hedge."

Snooper inspected the neat low hedge between the two burrows. His brow wrinkled deep in thought as an ambulance arrived. "Officer Beck, once Molly is safely away, cordon off the area. Let no one else in or out."

The otter saluted Snooper. "Yes, Detective."

Snooper shuffled off down the path. Sly skipped alongside him.

"This is *so* exciting!" she squealed. "Do you have any clue who did it?"

Snooper flicked a flea from his spines.

"Of course. It's obvious."

"Really?" exclaimed Sly, her tail all aquiver. "Who's your suspect?"

Snooper sighed. "You have the clues. Work it out for yourself."

"You're right. I won't learn if you have to tell me," replied Sly, studying her notes. "This is why you're the great Detective Snooper! I can't believe how lucky I am to be your partner. I know I requested it, but I thought there'd be a long waiting list—"

Snooper stopped in his tracks. "You *asked* to work with me?"

"Of course," replied Sly. "Whyever not? You solved the insolvable Case of the Cunning Caiman and the Mystery of the Mocking Magpie. You're a legend!"

Snooper tugged a worm from his pouch and popped it into his mouth. Sly grimaced.

"What's wrong?" said Snooper, chewing on the wriggling worm.

"Ermm … nothing," Sly replied, her stomach turning. She offered him an acorn from her knapsack.

"Wouldn't you rather have a healthy nut? Much better for the waistline!"

Snooper regarded the acorn as if it were a hand grenade, then glanced down at his bulging belly.

"My waistline is perfectly fine, thank you!"

Smiling awkwardly, Sly changed topics. "So how *did* you solve the Case of the Cunning Caiman?"

A dark shadow fell across Snooper's face. "I don't like talking about past cases!"

"N-no, of course not," Sly agreed. "You need to focus your mind on the current case. So, what's the plan?"

Snooper shuffled on. "I interview the suspect … and get a confession."

3 The Suspect

Curled in the corner of the glass cell was a long blue snake, his skin dull and dried out. As Snooper and Sly approached, the adder opened one clouded eye and hissed at them.

Sly edged nervously forward and whispered, "Good cop, bad cop routine?"

"What *are* you talking about?" muttered Snooper. "I ask the questions. You keep your mouth shut."

Sly nodded. "The silent treatment. Got it!"

Snooper rapped on the glass. "Ali! I'm charging you with the attempted murder of Molly Mouse. Do you have anything to say in your defence?"

The adder raised his head. "Ssssssnooper, you've got the wrong suspect ... *again*."

Snooper's snout twitched. "Are you sure about that? Molly's neighbour heard arguing and someone leave. *Someone* not tall enough to be seen over a very low hedge."

"Jussst because I ssslither on my ssstomach doesn't prove anything," spat Ali.

"True, but Molly's been bitten on the neck and poisoned ... plus I found *this* at the crime scene." Snooper held up a dull brown snake scale. "All the evidence points to *you*, Ali. Now confess."

The snake's tongue flicked out in annoyance. "I admit I had lunch with Molly but—"

"No, you wanted Molly *for* lunch!" interrupted Sly.

The snake glared at the squirrel. "If you let me finisssh ... I wasn't hungry."

"Tell that to the judge!" Sly laughed. "Everyone knows you like mice—"

"Sly!" warned Snooper. "Let me handle this …"

But Sly was just warming up to her role. "Admit it!" she said, pressing her nose against the glass. "You're a cold-blooded killer!"

Ali struck at Sly. His fangs cracked the glass, leaving two small holes.

Sly leapt away, her tail on end. "He t-t-t-ried to k-k-kill me!"

Snooper leant close to the glass and met Ali's glare. "You've given me all the proof I need."

4 The Chief Inspector

"That snake should be locked away for life!" said Sly, her tail still trembling as they mounted the steps to the police station.

Snooper was chewing hard on a worm.

"You saw how he lunged at me," Sly went on. "Murder in his evil eyes."

A large beaver waddled past. "You're alive then, Sly!" the detective sergeant said.

"Errr ... yes," she replied.

The beaver sucked on his large front teeth. "Impressive! You're surviving with Snooper longer than I'd have expected—"

15

Sly frowned as the detective sergeant waddled on. "What does he mean by that?"

"Nothing," mumbled Snooper, barging into the chief inspector's office without knocking.

The grey owl perched behind the desk looked up. "Snooper," chirped Octavia. "I trust this means you have Ali's confession?"

"No," replied Snooper.

Octavia peered over her spectacles. "*No?* Then why are you here?"

"He didn't do it."

OCTAVIA OWL

"*What?*" exclaimed Octavia and Sly together.

Octavia ruffled her feathers. "Ali is the prime suspect. He has motive, the means and the criminal history. You also have the proof in your hand! Now charge him and get this over with."

"I have a hunch—" Snooper began.

"Not another of your hair-brained hunches!" hooted Octavia. "I gave this case to you because it's clear cut."

"The evidence doesn't add up," insisted Snooper.

"We don't have time for you to ponder this case forever," Octavia screeched. "A mouse's life is on the line!"

"I realise that," said Snooper, "but I think—"

"Enough of what you think," snapped Octavia. "Time is running out."

"Give us 24 hours," Sly said.

Octavia glanced at the squirrel as if seeing her for the first time. "And you are?"

OCTAVIA OWL

Sly stood to attention. "Detective Sly! Snooper's new partner."

"Ah, the junior detective I hired!" smirked Octavia. "Unfortunately the victim doesn't have 24 hours."

"I only need 20," said Snooper.

Octavia clicked her beak in irritation. "All right, but *don't* make me regret this, Snooper!"

5 The Line-Up

"Sorry it took so long, Snooper, but
I've rounded up all your suspects,"
said Sly, proudly presenting
the line-up of a cat,
a bat, a scorpion
and a centipede.

"You disturbed me
from my catnap!"
yawned Artemis.

Snooper grabbed
the cat's open mouth.
"We value your cooperation,"
he said, as he put a ruler to
Artemis's teeth.

"Is this a dentist check-up?"
the scorpion snapped. "Because I
don't have teeth."

"No, Spike," said Snooper,
releasing Artemis. "But you do
have a stinger!"

"Yes, I do," snarled Spike.
"And one strike is all I need to stun you."

"That's good to know," said Snooper, moving on to the next suspect.

Blinking in the light, the bat demanded, "Why are we here at this unsocial time of day?"

Snooper examined Nora's sharp fangs. "Molly the Mouse was bitten in the neck and poisoned. I need to find out who did it... and quickly, if I'm to save her life!"

"But I'm not venomous," Nora protested.

"You're a vampire bat!" Sly said. "Of course you are."

Nora turned hungrily to Sly. "I may suck on blood, but I don't paralyse my prey with poison ... not like Cecil here."

The centipede's antennae twitched but he stayed silent.

"Fair point," agreed Snooper and rounded on the final suspect.

"What is that *awful* smell?" gagged Artemis, holding a paw to his nose.

Snooper pressed the centipede's head against the wall with his ruler.
"It's a centipede's defence mechanism. Their venom not only immobilises their prey, its stink wards off predators. They release it when they feel threatened."

Cecil's jaws snapped at Snooper, their sharp
points gleaming.

Sly pulled out a pair of handcuffs to arrest Cecil ... then
realised she probably needed a lot more handcuffs than two!

Without warning Snooper stormed out of the room.
Sly found him in the hallway chewing furiously on yet
another worm.

"So which one did it?" she asked.

"None of them!"

6 The Anti-Venom

Snooper paced the hospital corridor outside the emergency room where Doctor Brock and two vole nurses tended to Molly.

"What am I missing?" Snooper muttered to himself.

Sly scurried beside him, hands behind her back, brow furrowed, copying her hero.

Snooper reached into his pouch and discovered he'd run out of worms. He sucked on a dead flea instead, but it wasn't the same.

The chief inspector fluttered into the ward.

"Snooper, you're out of time."

"I know!" he shot back.

"Watch your tone, Detective," warned Octavia.

"Once more, your dallying has put an animal's life at risk!"

Knocking on the door, she got the doctor's attention.

"All evidence points to Ali the Adder as her attacker."

"Thank you, Chief Inspector," said Doctor Brock.

"Nurse, prep the snake anti-venom."

As the nurse filled a long syringe, Snooper paced faster. "But I'm sure it *isn't* Ali!"

"Who else could it be?" Octavia asked wearily.

"I don't know," replied Snooper, "but I think it's a grave mistake to use *snake* anti-venom."

Octavia's head rotated all the way round to look at him. "Snooper, if Doctor Brock doesn't administer anti-venom, Molly will die."

Snooper pulled fretfully at his spines. "And if he gives her the wrong one, she could die too! I've a strong hunch— "

"Your hunch is just a hunch," said Octavia. "I deal in facts – and those facts point to Ali."

Snooper was so deep in thought that he walked straight into Sly's tail coming the other way.

"Sorry," said Sly as Snooper spluttered fur.

He wiped angrily at his face. "What's this?" he said, examining the white sticky gunk on his hands.

He pulled out his magnifying glass and studied Sly's tail. Meanwhile, the nurse handed the doctor the syringe to inject the patient.

"STOP!" cried Snooper. "Molly *wasn't* bitten by a snake."

Then he rushed out of the hospital.

7 The Hidden Hunter

"I thought we were in a hurry," said Sly, as she jogged alongside Snooper.

"This *is* me in a hurry!" panted Snooper, waddling as fast as his stumpy legs would carry him.

They reached Molly's burrow where Officer Beck still stood guard. She saluted at their approach.

"Anyone … go in … or out?" gasped Snooper.

The officer shook her head.

"Then the attacker must still be inside," said Snooper.

Sly's eyes widened in alarm. "*Still inside?*"

Sly swallowed nervously as she crept into the burrow behind Snooper. All was dark and shadowy. Aside from the removal of Molly's body, nothing else had changed. The picture lay in the corner, its frame broken. The vase sat untouched on the sideboard. And smashed plates and cutlery littered the floor.

"I know you're here," Snooper called out. "And I know you did it... show yourself, Vesper!"

A black shadow leapt from behind the sideboard. Snooper rolled instinctively into a ball, using his spines to fend off the attacker.

Sly squealed as the horrifying creature now sprung at her. In a panic, she whacked it with her tail. The shadow flew across the room and hit the wall.

Snooper uncurled and, with surprising speed, threw several of his loose spines to pin the stunned creature.

"Just as I suspected," said Snooper.
"Vesper the Hunting Spider."

Sly peered warily at the squirming creature. "How did you know?"

"No time for explanations," replied Snooper, turning for the door. "Doctor Brock needs to know it was *spider* venom. We must get back to the hospital, fast!"

Leaving Officer Beck to guard the prisoner, they raced off. But Snooper wasn't built for speed, and he'd eaten far too many worms. Legs buckling, he collapsed in the dirt. "*Fleabags!*" he gasped. "We won't make it in time."

"You may not, but I can," said Sly, and she sprinted on ahead.

Sly arrived at the hospital with only seconds to spare. "Use spider anti-venom!" she told Doctor Brock.

Quickly, he injected the correct medicine. Several tense minutes passed …

Then, just as a wheezing and red-faced Snooper lumbered in, Molly's eyes flickered open.

"Oh, hello, Snooper!" said Molly brightly. "Are you all right? You look like you need a doctor!"

Everyone in the room laughed.

8 The Vital Clue

"I ssssaid you had the wrong one," hissed Ali, as he slid past Snooper and Sly outside the police station.

"Be grateful," Snooper grunted. "*I'm* the one who proved your innocence."

"You only proved you're a bumbling idiot!" spat Ali, then glared at Sly. "No glassss between ussss now!"

Sly kept safely behind Snooper's spines as Ali slithered away, his skin glistening and his eyes bright.

"There's no pleasing some animals!" Sly called after the snake. Once Ali had gone, Sly asked Snooper, "So how did you figure out this case?"

Snooper pulled a fresh worm from his pouch and chewed contentedly. "Well ... the bite mark, poisoning and snake scale did all point to Ali. He even admitted having lunch with Molly around the time of the attack. But he also said he wasn't hungry ... and I believed him. His skin was dull and dry and his eyes were clouded – signs he was moulting. When a snake is about to shed its skin, it doesn't eat."

"*Really?*" said Sly. "He looked hungry just then."

Snooper smirked. "That's because he's shed his skin now."

"And *that* was your proof?"

"No, it was when he attacked you," revealed Snooper. "The holes in the glass proved his fangs were too wide to leave the bite marks on Molly's neck. So were Artemis the Cat's."

"My line-up!" said Sly, proudly puffing out her chest at her part in the investigation.

Snooper nodded. "Spike boasted he could stun me in one strike – so why would he have needed to sting Molly twice? Nora pointed out that vampire bats aren't venomous. That left Cecil …" He slurped on his worm. "For a moment I believed I had the culprit. But a centipede's jaws bite sideways and are too small to match Molly's wound. I hit a dead-end …"

"So what led you to Vesper?" asked Sly.

Snooper glanced at Sly. "The vital clue was with us all along... on your tail! When you barged in on the crime scene, your tail must've swept up her cobwebs."

Sly hung her head in shame. "So it's *my* fault you didn't solve it earlier ..."

"Don't blame yourself," Snooper said, adjusting his glasses. "With my poor eyesight, I might never have spotted the cobweb ... unless it was right in my face!"

He chortled and Sly found herself laughing too as the chief inspector flew down from her office.

"Seems your hunch proved right, Snooper," she hooted. "But you cut it rather close! Luckily for you, your partner is quick. Good work, Sly. Your speed saved Molly's life."

Sly grinned and danced on her hind legs. "Tada!"

Snooper frowned at her. "What was that for?"

"To celebrate solving our first case *together*," said Sly, "as The Animal Detective Agents ... TADA!"

Sly's Sleuth Diary

What a thrilling first day on the job!

A poisoned mouse. No weapon. No footprints.
A frantic race to save the victim's life. And I'm partnered
with the legendary Detective Snooper!
Can it get any better?

It was touch and go whether we'd discover
the attacker in time. All the clues pointed to
Ali the Adder. But Snooper's amazing powers of
deduction proved his innocence and he uncovered the real
criminal behind the attack …

Vesper the Hunting Spider!

If it wasn't for the fact that I was so clumsy and
Snooper had bumped into my tail, we may never have
discovered the truth.

Luckily, I was fast enough to deliver the news to
Doctor Brock and Molly survived!

It's amazing to be working with the great
Detective Snooper. But why won't he talk about
past cases? And I wonder what our next case will be …?

 Ideas for reading

Written by Gill Matthews
Primary Literacy Consultant

Reading objectives:
- check that the text makes sense, discuss understanding and explain the meaning of words in context
- ask questions to improve understanding
- draw inferences such as inferring characters' feelings, thoughts and motives from their actions, and justify inferences with evidence

Spoken language objectives:
- articulate and justify answers, arguments and opinions
- participate in discussions, presentations, performances, role play, improvisations and debates

Curriculum links: Science – Living things and their habitats

Interest words: sheepishly, squealed, awkwardly, edged

Resources: ICT, books about animals that are featured in the book, A3 paper, marker pens

Build a context for reading

- Read and discuss the title. Ask children what an adder is. Draw attention to the sign on the front cover. Encourage children to predict what the book might be about.
- Read the back cover blurb. How does this help with predictions about the story?
- Check children's understanding of the final sentence of the blurb.

Understand and apply reading strategies

- Read Chapter 1 aloud together using the meaning, punctuation and dialogue to help you read with expression.
- Discuss what impression children get of the two characters. Encourage them to refer to the text to justify their responses.
- Ask children to read Chapters 2 and 3, focussing on the evidence that Snooper collects. Discuss their findings, checking on their understanding of what they have read.